This Book Belongs To:

_____

Thank you for trying out our Sweet & Cute Kawaii Coloring Book!

Get ready to dive into 50 super cute and fun illustrations that will make your coloring time a blast. Download & Color these pages as many times as you'd like.

ABOUT US

We're all about the cute and cozy vibes here at Lulu Drake Coloring, and we created this book just for you to share in the fun!

Don't miss out on more of our coloring books and awesome downloads at luludrake.com.

Join the fun on TikTok and Instagram by following us @luludrakecoloring, and show off your amazing pages using #luludrakecoloring!

We have even more fun products at: LuluDrake.com

@luludrakecoloring

LuluDrake.com   @LuluDrakeColoring

LuluDrake.com @LuluDrakeColoring

LuluDrake.com @LuluDrakeColoring

LuluDrake.com   @LuluDrakeColoring

If you enjoyed this book, check out our other great books and products at LuluDrake.com

Get 20 FREE Coloring Pages Here!

Made in the USA
Monee, IL
10 October 2024

67508818R00059